Pippi's Extraordinary Ordinary Day

The text in this book has been excerpted,
with Astrid Lindgren's assistance,
from two chapters in *Pippi Longstocking*.

PUFFIN BOOKS
Published by the Penguin Group
Penguin Putnam Books for Young Readers,
345 Hudson Street, New York, New York, 10014, U.S.A.
Penguin Books Ltd, 27 Wrights Lane, London W8 5T7, England
Penguin Books Australia Ltd, Ringwood, Victoria, Australia
Penguin Books Canada Ltd, 10 Alcorn Avenue, Toronto, Ontario,
Canada M4V 3B2
Penguin Books (N.Z.) Ltd, 182-190 Wairau Road, Auckland 10,
New Zealand
Penguin Books Ltd, Registered Offices: Harmondsworth,
Middlesex, England

This edition first published in the United States of America by
Viking, a division of Penguin Putnam Books for Young Readers,
1999
Published by Puffin Books,
a division of Penguin Putnam Books for Young Readers, 2001

10 9 8 7 6 5 4 3 2 1

Text copyright © The Viking Press, Inc., 1950
Copyright renewed Viking Penguin, Inc., 1978
Illustrations copyright © Michael Chesworth, 1999
All rights reserved

THE LIBRARY OF CONGRESS HAS CATALOGED THE VIKING EDITION AS FOLLOWS:
Lindgren, Astrid, date
Pippi's extraordinary ordinary day / by Astrid Lindgren ; pictures by
Michael Chesworth.

Summary: When her friends Tommy and Annika have a day off from
school, Pippi takes them on a far from ordinary picnic.
ISBN 0-670-88073-6
[1. Picnicking Fiction. 2. Sweden Fiction.]
I. Chesworth, Michael, ill. II. Title. III. Series: Lindgren, Astrid, date
Pippi Longstocking storybook.
PZ7.L65585Po 1999 [E]—dc21 99-26986 CIP

Puffin Books ISBN 0-14-056841-7

Printed in the United States of America

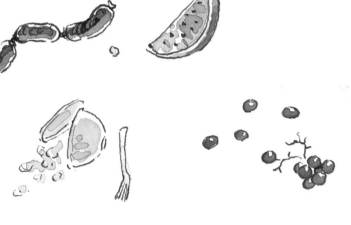

Pippi's Extraordinary Ordinary Day

by Astrid Lindgren
pictures by Michael Chesworth

PUFFIN BOOKS

Way out at the end of a tiny little town was an old overgrown garden, and in the garden was an old house, and in the house lived Pippi Longstocking. She was nine years old, and she lived there all alone. She had no mother and no father, and that was of course very nice because there was no one to tell her to go to bed just when she was having the most fun, and no one who could make her take cod liver oil when she much preferred caramel candy.

Once upon a time Pippi had had a father of whom she was extremely fond. He was a sea captain who sailed on the great ocean, and Pippi had sailed with him in his ship until one day her father was blown overboard in a storm and disappeared. But Pippi was absolutely certain he would come back.

Her father had bought the old house in the garden many years ago. While Pippi was waiting for him to come back she went straight home to live at Villa Villekulla. That was the name of the house.

Two things Pippi took with her from the ship: a little monkey whose name was Mr. Nilsson—he was a present from her father—and a big suitcase full of gold pieces. Pippi also had a horse of her own that she had bought with one of her many gold pieces the day she came home to Villa Villekulla.

Beside Villa Villekulla was another garden and another house. In that house lived a father and mother and two charming children, Tommy and Annika, who often wished for a playmate. And when Pippi Longstocking moved next door, they got the best playmate any child could wish for. This is the story of one of their adventures together. . . .

"We don't have any school today because we're having Scrubbing Vacation while they clean the school," said Tommy to Pippi.

"Scrubbing Vacation? Well, I like that!" said Pippi. "Another injustice! Do I get any Scrubbing Vacation? Indeed I don't, though goodness knows I need one. Just look at the kitchen floor. But for that matter," she added, "now I come to think of it, I can scrub without any vacation. And that's what I intend to do right now, Scrubbing Vacation or no Scrubbing Vacation. I'd like to see anybody stop me! You two sit on the kitchen table, out of the way."

Pippi heated a big kettle of water and without more ado poured it out on the kitchen floor. She took off her big shoes and laid them neatly on the bread plate. She tied two scrubbing brushes on her feet and skated over the floor, plowing through the water so that it splashed all around her.

"I certainly should have been a skating princess," she said and kicked her left foot up so high that the scrubbing brush broke a piece out of the overhead light.

"Grace and charm I have at least," she continued and skipped nimbly over a chair standing in her way.

"Well, now I guess it's clean," she said at last and took off the brushes.

"Aren't you going to dry the floor?" asked Annika.

"Oh, no, it can dry in the sun," answered Pippi. "I don't think it will catch cold so long as it keeps moving."

Tommy and Annika climbed down from the table and stepped across the floor very carefully so they wouldn't get wet.

Out of doors the sun shone in a clear blue sky. It was one of those radiant September days that make you feel like walking in the woods. Pippi had an idea.

"Let's take Mr. Nilsson and go on a little picnic."

"Oh, yes, let's," cried Tommy and Annika.

Tommy and Annika rushed home to ask their mother, and when they came back Pippi was waiting by the gate with Mr. Nilsson on her shoulder, a walking stick in one hand, and a big basket in the other.

The children walked along the road a little way and then turned into a pasture where a pleasant path wound in and out among the thickets of birch and hazel.

Presently they came to a gate on the other side of which was an even more beautiful pasture, but right in front of the gate stood a cow who looked as if nothing would persuade her to move. Annika yelled at her, and Tommy bravely went up and tried to push her away, but she just stood there staring at the children with her big cow eyes. To put an end to the matter, Pippi set down her basket and lifted the cow out of the way. The cow, looking very silly, lumbered off into the hazel bushes.

"How can cows be so bull-headed," said Pippi and jumped over the gate.

"What a lovely, lovely wood!" cried Annika in delight as she climbed up on all the stones she could see. Tommy had brought along a dagger Pippi had given him, and with it he cut walking sticks for Annika and for himself. He cut his thumb a little too, but that didn't matter.

"What have you got in your basket?" asked Annika. "Is it something good?"

"I wouldn't tell you for a thousand dollars," said Pippi. "First we must find a good picnic spot."

Tommy found a little clearing among the hazel bushes, and he thought that would be a good place.

"Oh, no, that's not sunny enough for my freckles," said Pippi, "and I do think freckles are so attractive."

Farther on they came to a hill that was easy to climb. On one side of the hill was a nice sunny rock just like a little balcony, and there they sat down.

"Now shut your eyes while I set the table," said Pippi. Tommy and Annika squeezed their eyes as tightly shut as possible. They heard Pippi opening the basket and rattling paper.

"One, two, nineteen—now you may look," said Pippi at last.

They looked, and they squealed with delight when

they saw all the good things Pippi had spread on the ground. There were good sandwiches with meatballs and ham, a whole pile of sugared pancakes, several little brown sausages, and three pineapple puddings. For, you see, Pippi had learned cooking from the cook on her father's ship.

"Aren't Scrubbing Vacations great?" said Tommy with his mouth full of pancakes. "We ought to have them every day."

"No, indeed, I'm not that anxious to scrub," said Pippi. "It's fun, to be sure, but not every day. That would be too tiresome."

At last the children were so full they could hardly move, and they sat still in the sunshine and just enjoyed it.

"I wonder if it is hard to fly," said Pippi and looked dreamily over the edge of the rock. The rock sloped down very steeply below them, and it was a long way to the ground.

"Down at least one ought to be able to learn to fly," she continued. "It must be harder to fly up. But you could begin with the easiest way. I do think I'll try."

"No, Pippi," cried both Tommy and Annika. "Oh, dear, Pippi, don't do that!"

But Pippi was already standing at the edge.

"Fly, you foolish fly, fly, and the foolish fly flew," she said, and just as she said "flew" she lifted her arms and took off into the air. In half a second there was a thud. It was Pippi hitting the ground. Tommy and Annika lay on their stomachs and looked down at her, terrified.

Pippi got up and brushed off her knees. "I forgot to flap," she said joyfully, "and I guess I had too many pancakes in my stomach."

At that moment the children noticed that Mr. Nilsson had disappeared. He had evidently gone off on a little expedition of his own.

Pippi was so angry that she threw her shoe into a big deep pool of water. "You should never take monkeys with you anywhere," she said. "He should have been left at home to pick fleas off the horse. That would have served him right," she continued, wading out into the pool to get her shoe. The water reached up to her waist.

"I might as well take advantage of this and wash my hair," said Pippi and ducked her head under the water and kept it there so long that the water began to bubble.

"There now, I've saved a visit to the hairdresser," she said contentedly when at last she came up for air. She stepped out of the pool and put on her shoe. Then they went off to hunt for Mr. Nilsson.

"Hear how it squishes when I walk," laughed Pippi. "It says 'klafs, klafs' in my dress and 'squish, squish' in my shoes. Isn't that funny?

"Mr. Nilsson certainly can be exasperating," Pippi continued. "He's always doing things like this. Once in Arabia he ran away from me and took a position as a maidservant to an elderly widow. That last was a lie, of course," she added after a pause.

Tommy suggested they all three go in different directions and hunt. At first Annika didn't want to because she was a little afraid, but Tommy said, "You aren't a 'fraidy cat, are you?" And, of course, Annika couldn't tolerate such an insult, so off they all went.

Tommy went through a field. Mr. Nilsson he did

not find, but he did find something else. A bull! Or to be more exact, the bull found Tommy. And the bull did not like Tommy, for he was a very cross bull who was not at all fond of children. With his head down he charged toward Tommy, bellowing fearfully. Tommy let out a terrified shriek that could be heard all through the woods. Pippi and Annika heard it and came running to see what was the matter. By that time the bull had almost reached Tommy who had fallen head over heels over a stump.

"What a stupid bull!" said Pippi to Annika, who was crying uncontrollably. "He ought to know he can't act like that. He'll get Tommy's white sailor suit all dirty. I'll have to go and talk some sense into the stupid animal."

And off she started. She ran up and pulled the bull by the tail. "Forgive me for breaking up the party," she said. Since she had given his tail a good hard pull, the bull turned around and saw a new child to catch on his horns.

"As I was saying," went on Pippi, "forgive me for breaking up, and also forgive me for breaking off," and with that she broke off one of the bull's horns. "It isn't the style to have two horns this year," she said. "All the better bulls have just one horn—if any." And she broke off the other horn too.

As bulls have no feeling in their horns, this one
didn't know what she had done. He charged at Pippi,
and if she had been any other child there would have
been nothing left but a grease spot.

"Hey, hey, stop tickling me!" shrieked Pippi. "You
can't imagine how ticklish I am! Hey, stop, stop, or
I'll die laughing!"

But the bull didn't stop, and at last Pippi jumped up on his back to get a little rest. To be sure, she didn't get much, because the bull didn't in the least approve of having Pippi on his back. He dodged about madly to get her off, but she clamped her knees and hung on. The bull dashed up and down the field, bellowing so hard that smoke came out of

his nostrils. Pippi laughed and shrieked and waved at Tommy and Annika, who stood a little distance away, trembling like aspen leaves. The bull whirled round and round, trying to throw Pippi.

"See me dancing with my little friend!" cried Pippi and kept her seat. At last the bull was so tired

that he lay down on the ground and wished that he'd never seen such a thing as a child. He had never thought children amounted to much anyway.

"Are you going to take a little nap now?" asked Pippi politely. "Then I won't disturb you."

She got off his back and
went over to Tommy and
Annika. Tommy had cried a
little. He had a cut on one
arm, but Annika had ban-
daged it with her handkerchief
so that it no longer hurt.

"Oh, Pippi!" cried Annika excitedly.

"Sh, sh," whispered Pippi. "Don't wake the bull.
He's sleeping. If we wake him he'll be fussy."

But the next minute, without paying any attention
to the bull and his nap, she was shrieking at the top
of her voice, "Mr. Nilsson, Mr. Nilsson, where are
you? We've got to go home."

And, believe it or not, there sat Mr. Nilsson up in a pine tree, sucking his tail and looking very lonely. It wasn't much fun for a little monkey to be left all alone in the woods. He skipped down from the pine and up on Pippi's shoulder, waving his little straw hat as he always did when he was very happy.

"Well, well, so you aren't going to be a maidservant this time?" said Pippi, stroking his back. "Oh, that was a lie, that's true," she continued. "But still, if it's true, how can it be a lie?" she argued. "You wait and see, it's going to turn out that he was a maidservant in Arabia after all, and if that's the case, I know who's going to make the meatballs at our house hereafter!"

And then they strolled home, Pippi's dress still going "klafs, klafs," and her shoes "squish, squish."

Tommy and Annika thought they had had a wonderful day in spite of the bull, and they sang a song they had learned at school. It was really a summer song, but they thought it fitted very well even if it was now nearly autumn:

In the happy summertime
Through field and wood we make our way.
Nobody's sad, everyone's gay.
We sing as we go, hol-lá, hol-ló!

You who are young,
Come join in our song.
Don't sit home moping all the day long.
We sing as we go, hol-lá, hol-ló.

Pippi sang too, but with slightly different words:

In the happy summertime
Through field and wood I make my way.
I do exactly as I wish,
And when I walk it goes squish, squish,
Squish, squish. Squish, squish.

And my old shoe—
It's really true—
Sometimes says "chip" and sometimes "choo."
For the shoe is wet.
The bull sleeps yet.
And I eat all the dessert I can get.
In the happy summertime
I squish wherever I go. Squish-oh! Squish-oh!